CARS AT PLAY

written by Rick and Ann Walton

illustrated by James Lee Croft

G. P. PUTNAM'S SONS

NEW YORK

Library of Congress Cataloging-in-Publication Data Walton, Rick. Cars at play / written by Rick Walton and Ann Walton; illustrated by James Lee Croft. p. cm. Summary: Rhymed text and illustrations show all the things that cars do when they play. [1. Automobiles—Fiction. 2. Play—Fiction. 3. Stories in rhyme.] I. Walton, Ann, 1963- II. Croft, James, 1970- ill. III. Title. PZ8.3.W199 Car 2002 [E]—dc21 00-055250 ISBN 0-399-23599-X   10 9 8 7 6 5 4 3 2 1
First Impression

Cars play leapfrog,

Cars go wading,

Cars play
hide
-and-
seek,

FIZZ

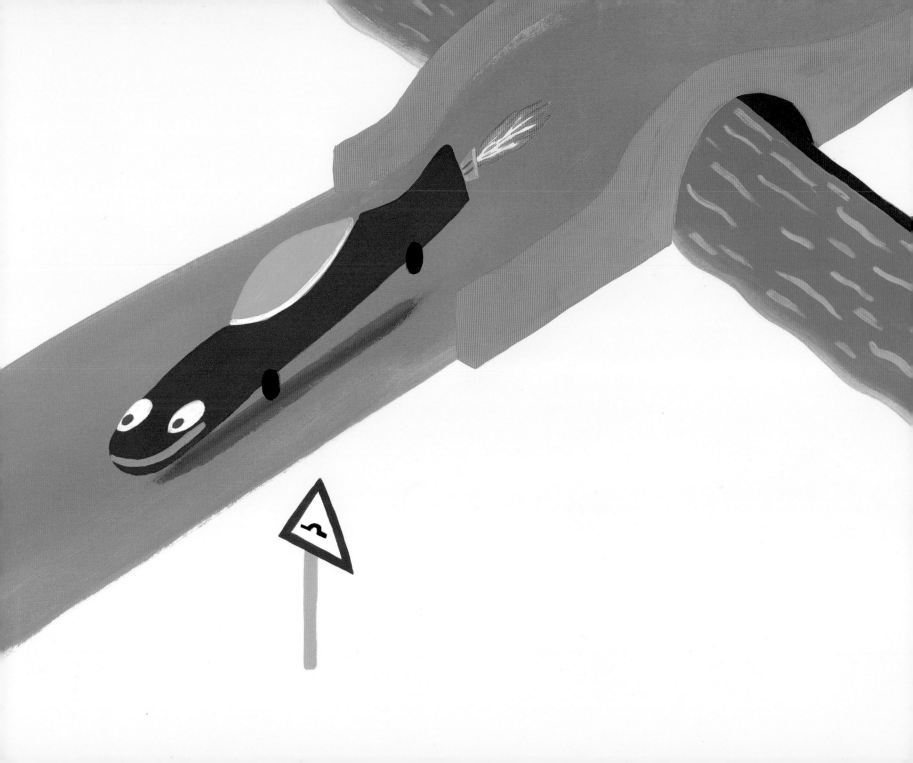

And go ice-skating.

Cars play piggy back,

Cars
play
jacks,

Cars play dodgeball,

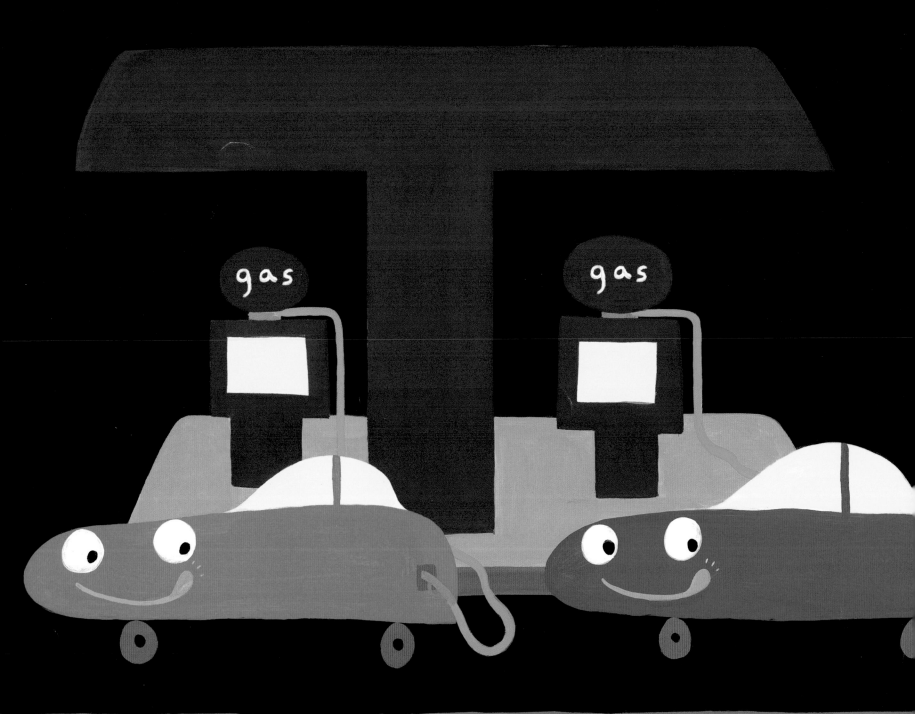

Then
eat
snacks.

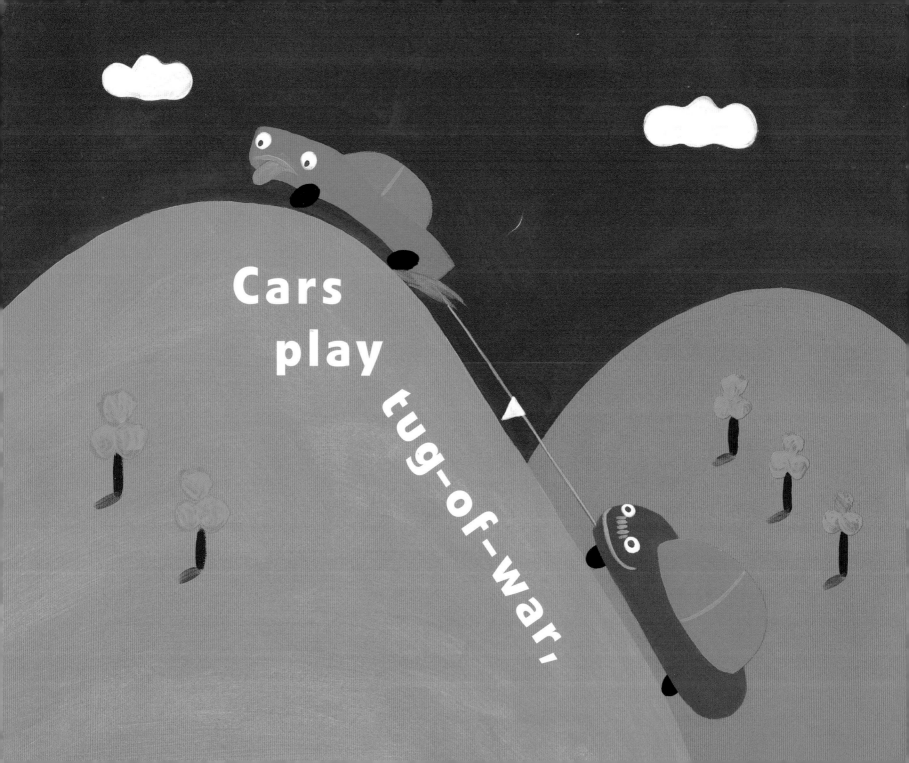

Cars play tug-of-war,

Cars play in the mud,

Some cars swing.

Cars play
Simon Says,

Cars play dress up,

bumper cars

Cars have fun!

hall of
mirrors